THE ADVENTURES OF
Laila and Ahmed in Syria

Written by Nushin Alloo | Illustrated by Shadia Kassem

Published by

BEAUTY BENEATH THE RUBBLE
CHANGE THE NARRATIVE TO CHANGE THE FUTURE

Copyright © 2018 by Nushin Alloo
Illustrations by Shadia Kassem
Design by Maece Seirafi

Printed in the United States of America
First Printing, 2018

ISBN: 978-0-692-11094-2

Library of Congress Control Number: 2018904799

Published by:

BEAUTY BENEATH
THE RUBBLE

beneaththerubble.org

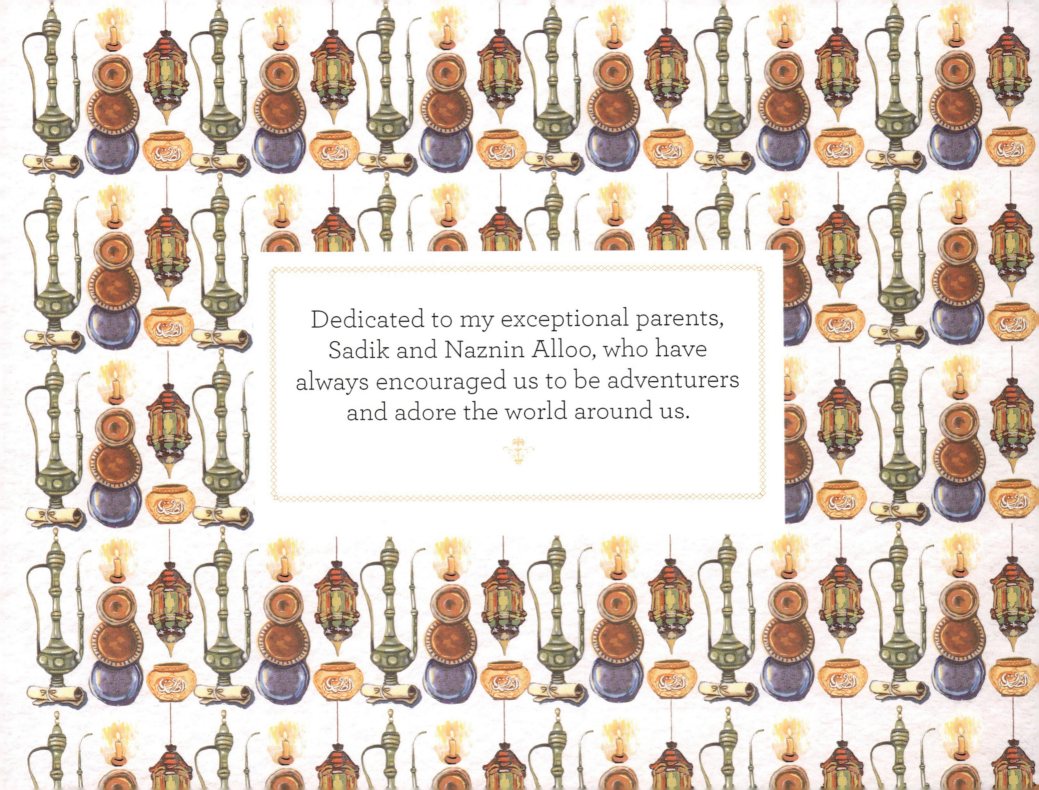

Dedicated to my exceptional parents,
Sadik and Naznin Alloo, who have
always encouraged us to be adventurers
and adore the world around us.

Have you ever looked at a map and wanted
to jump right into it? Think of all the places
you would see and the adventures you could
have. But that is just not possible...
or is it?

· · 1 · ·

ONE

Although she was only ten years old, Laila had always wished she could jump into a map and go on a wild adventure. "My grandfather was the world's greatest traveler," she would say to her friends. "He visited over forty countries, and one day *I* will do the same."

Laila would dream of all the places she would see and all the people she would meet. But she didn't want to wait to be grown up to do this; she wanted to go *now*.

"Damascus, Somalia, Mali and Spain.
China, Sri Lanka, Iraq and Bahrain,"
she'd sing to herself.

On the other hand, Laila's younger brother Ahmed was not like her at all. No—he loved to stay home, and if the family went out together he would hold on tightly to his mama's hand while hugging his soft, white blanket. Any thought of leaving home made him nervous.

 **T W O**

One morning while Mama was away, Laila tiptoed into her parents' room to look for a very special treasure, a book her grandfather had given to her mama many years ago. She persuaded Ahmed to help her, although he didn't want to.

"Ahmed, come help me!" she insisted.

"Do I have to?" he whined back.

Laila searched for hours and hours, with just a little help from Ahmed.

I hope Mama won't mind us doing this, she thought as she opened the drawers next to her parents' bed, *but I need to find that book. I can't wait anymore.*

She climbed up to look on the highest shelf in the closet, knelt to peek under the bed, searched in old boxes. She looked *everywhere*, but she couldn't find it. As she was about to give up, she remembered her parents talking about a secret compartment in the carved wooden chest in their bedroom. Laila gasped. There it was.

"I found it! I found it!" She jumped up and down, hugging the book to her chest. Her smile stretched from ear to ear.

The cover said *Rihla* by Ibn Battuta.

Ahmed scratched his head, confused. "What is it?" he said, trying to peer over her shoulder. "A book? What is so exciting about a book?"

Laila frowned. "Ahmed, this is not just *any* old book. It's *Rihla*, Grandpa's travel journal, where he wrote about all his adventures from Morocco to China, and…it's magical."

T H R E E

Inside, it was filled with drawings, stories, and maps of all the places Grandpa had ever visited.

Laila read the first page her grandfather wrote.

"I set out alone, with no friend to bring me cheer or group to join, but with a strong desire inside me to travel, so I left my home as birds leave their nest."

Wow, he was just like me, Laila thought. As she hurried to flip to the next page, a crumpled sheet of paper slipped out and fell onto her lap.

"What's this?" Laila asked. She read it aloud:

My dearest grandchildren, I'm so proud of you.
Now it's time for you to see the world, too.
I've planted some clues to lend you a hand,
they lead to a gift in a faraway land.
Begin at the castle to find your first clue,
and know that my blessings will travel with you.

Love, Grandpa

P.S. Here's a hint: look for a helping hump.

FOUR

Laila's mind raced. "What does this mean?" she wondered. "Clues—castles—humps?"

Ahmed was about to ask the same question when a soft, glowing light floated in through the window, filling the room with a golden haze.

Ahmed edged back, closer to the wall, pointing at the light. "Laila, what is that? Is—is it going to hurt us?" he asked, clutching his white blanket close to his face.

Laila looked up in amazement.

"I don't think so, Ahmed. I think this is from Grandpa's book. I knew the book was magical!"

The children watched as the light took the shape of a ball and moved closer to them. It then hovered above their heads, just for a moment, before floating down and landing right on the book.

My dearest grandchildren, I'm so proud of you,
Now it's time for you to see the world, too.
I've planted some clues to lend you a hand,
they lead to a gift in a faraway land.
Begin at the castle to find your first clue,
and know that my blessings will travel with you.

Love, Grandpa

P.S. Here's a hint: look for a helping bump.

9

Suddenly a bright beam shot up and out from the book, like a fountain of fireworks. The book shivered, shook, and rose gently off the ground. Laila and Ahmed squealed and tried to cover their eyes with their hands.

"Ahhh! What's happening?" Ahmed cried as the open book grew bigger and bigger and *bigger,* until it reached the ceiling. Before Laila could answer, the light faded away to reveal a giant, open doorway.

Laila's eyes opened as wide as the doorway. "I can't believe this!" Her heart was beating so fast it felt like it was going to jump right out of her chest!

She leapt to her feet and tiptoed to the door to peek through. Grandpa's book had just become the entrance to a whole new world!

"I–I don't like this very much. I want Mama," said Ahmed, taking a small step backwards.

"Ahmed, don't be afraid," Laila urged him. "This must be what Grandpa was talking about in his note." She held up the note for him to see. "He left a gift for us to find on the other side of that doorway. It will be an adventure. Think of the treasure we'll find and the food we'll eat. I know you'll love it. Come on...let's go!"

"But shouldn't we tell Mama and Baba?" Ahmed asked as he continued to creep backwards, trying to get away. His parents always kept him safe when he was scared.

"We'll tell them all about it when we come back, I promise," Laila assured him. With that, she grabbed Ahmed's hand and pulled him with her through the doorway, not knowing where it would lead.

"Aaaaah!" the children shouted as they were swished and swirled through the door, spiraling downward and far, far away from home.

Thump! They landed on soft, powdery sand. The book landed right beside them.

Laila turned her head slowly from left to right and back again. "Where are we?"

❦ ·· FIVE ·· ❦

Laila and Ahmed scrambled to their feet, dusting the sand from their arms and legs. Ahmed sniffled and wiped his nose on the sleeve of his shirt. "I don't like this at all. I want to go home—and I dropped my blankey somewhere."

"Oh no, no, *no*." Laila shook her head. "We can't go home yet. Our adventure has just begun. This is exciting, isn't it? We need to find out where we are, and we need to solve Grandpa's clue to find the treasure he's left for us." She waved the book at Ahmed, reminding him that they already had a good map *and* the first clue. As she did, she saw someone in the distance coming closer.

"Do you see that man over there? He has two camels with him!" She jumped up and down. "That's it! Grandpa's letter said to look for the *helping hump*."

"So?" said Ahmed. "I see the man, but what does he have to do with helping humps?"

"Well, camels have humps, don't they? Maybe this man can help us find the castle!"

"Hmm...do you really think he will help us? We don't even know him." Ahmed frowned. "And how do we know that Grandpa was talking about camels?"

"There's no time to worry about what he might have meant. Let's talk to the man and see," said Laila, waving to the man. He saw her and smiled. Laila hurried toward him with Ahmed following closely behind her.

"Excuse me, sir. I'm Laila. My brother and I need to go to a castle, but we don't know where it is. We think we are supposed to travel on the backs of camels. Can you tell us the way, or where we might find some camels to help us?"

"*Ahlan wa sahlan*, welcome," the man said, smiling.

"I'd be happy to help you. We love having visitors here in Syria." He thought for a moment, rubbing his chin.

Syria? thought Laila. *So that's where the book has taken us.* Laila remembered how her grandfather, Ibn Battuta, had spent many years in Syria on his way to Mecca.

"We have the most magnificent castle not too far away," the man continued. "It could be the one you are looking for."

Laila was very happy to hear him say that. "How far is it?" she asked excitedly.

"Hmm...a bit too far to travel on foot, that is for sure." He then tapped his head again, thinking hard. "Aha!" he exclaimed after some time. "Here." He handed Laila one end of the long ropes that were tied around the camels' necks. "Something tells me you need my camels more than I do at the moment. I hope they will serve you well!"

Laila took the ropes in her hand, amazed by his kindness. "Really? Are you sure?"

The man chuckled. "Of course I am, dear girl. I am a *Bedouin*, a person of the desert. We love to help our guests. Here in the empty desert, we must help one another. Now take good care of them. You're lucky, these humps are full of water. A camel can survive months without water in this hot desert."

As Laila looked up at the camels' lovely long eyelashes, she saw a sparkle in their eyes. The man leaned down and whispered to her, "These are not ordinary camels, my dear. They are very intelligent and always know where they are going. They can take you wherever you want to go. You just say the word. When your adventure is over, the camels will find their way back to me."

One of the tall camels knelt down to let the children climb onto its back. Its hump was covered by colorful cloths and a saddle.

Laila jumped onto the back of one of the camels. Ahmed shook his head. "Uh-uh—I'm not riding on that! Those humps are too high."

"Come on, Ahmed! Don't be a scaredy-camel!" Laila teased, chuckling to herself. The camel began to trot forward, but she pulled it back. Not wanting to be left behind, Ahmed finally mustered the courage to jump onto the camel as well.

"Hmm...this is not so bad," he finally said, looking around from his perch on top of the camel's hump. "Wow...I can see so far!"

"Ready?" the man asked.

"Yes, I've been waiting for this my whole life. Let's go!" In her excitement, Laila bounced up and down in the saddle, then grabbed on tight.

"Take them to the castle, please," the man instructed his camels. He then turned to the children and said, "Don't worry, my camels will take care of the directions. Good luck on your adventure!"

The children thanked the man and waved him goodbye, as their camels set off toward the sun.

"Oh," the man called out before they had gone too far, "take good care of your grandpa's book. You're going need it!" He winked.

"What? How does he know about Grandpa's book?" Ahmed and Laila turned to each other and asked as the man slowly walked away into the golden sands of the desert.

SIX

The journey did not take long. They left the hot desert sand behind them and came to a large hill covered with grass and sweet-smelling flowers. On top of the hill was a mighty castle.

This must be it, Laila thought, *the castle from Grandpa's clue.*

The children slid off the camel's back and looked with amazement at the castle.

"I've seen this before!" Laila exclaimed. She grabbed Grandpa's book and flipped through the pages until she saw a picture of the same castle. She read aloud to Ahmed. "It says here that this castle was built by Crusaders hundreds of years ago, and it fit as many as two thousand soldiers inside its walls."

Ahmed wasn't listening. He was in his own little world. "This is the biggest building I've ever seen," he whispered to himself, tilting his head so far back that he almost fell over. He wanted to go inside and explore, but he was a little nervous being so far from home. He closed his eyes tightly for a moment, squeezing his fists. When he opened them, he ran straight up the hill and right into the castle without looking back.

"Ahmed, wait for me!" Laila yelled, running to catch up with him.

The halls were dark and narrow. Lanterns hung from the tall, curved ceilings. There were little windows everywhere that let in soft beams of light. Laila and Ahmed walked through the old kitchen, the stables, and the dining room where all the soldiers would eat. The castle was so huge and its halls were so long, the children thought it would never end.

Ahmed saw something shiny hanging from one of the stones in the wall. He stopped to look at it closely, but it was so high up, he couldn't quite reach it.

Laila ran up behind him. "What is that?"

"I think this might be our next clue," said Ahmed. He jumped and jumped and *jumped* and finally snatched it down and handed it to Laila.

"Wow, Ahmed, good job." Laila smiled she read the clue aloud:

In Syria's oldest city you will find
a market that is one of a kind.
It was once part of the ancient Silk Road;
there you will find your next clue to decode.
In the market you'll see a traveling shop,
your next clue will be waiting on top.

"A *traveling* shop? But there's no such thing," said Ahmed, scratching his head.

"Oldest city...oldest city..." Laila muttered to herself as she looked through all the colorful pages in Grandpa's book. "Aha! Here it is! It's called Aleppo, and it's one of the oldest cities in the world."

"But..." said Ahmed, "do we have to go to another place? I thought we were going to find whatever you are looking for here, in this castle." He sulked. "I want to go home."

"Come on, Ahmed—we must hurry," Laila interrupted, beginning to walk away. But as she stepped forward, she could not remember which way to go. "Uh-oh," she said with a frown, looking up and down the halls of the castle.

"What's wrong?" asked Ahmed.

"Umm...nothing. Let's go this way." She pointed to the left. She took a step forward then stopped. "Or maybe it's that way?" She looked to the right.

"What? Do you mean you don't know which way is out?" said Ahmed.

"It's just that this castle is so big...and we walked through so many rooms..." Laila said in an uncertain tone, fidgeting and feeling flustered. *What kind of an adventurer gets lost?* she thought. "What now?" she asked Ahmed, giving up.

Ahmed wanted to help. "I think I can remember the way," said Ahmed.

"How? There are so many hallways."

"I remember the things we saw when we came in. Like that window, I remember how I liked the blue and green glass in it..." He walked in the direction of the window. "And that doorway with the lantern..."

Ahmed retraced each step they had taken, and in no time he led them back to their camels.

"Wow, I did it!" exclaimed Ahmed, hoping Laila was proud of him.

"You sure did." Laila smiled, looking down and fidgeting a bit. She was feeling a little embarrassed that she had lost her way, but didn't want Ahmed to know. She jumped onto the camel. "Take us to Aleppo, please, camels!"

Off they went to Aleppo to search for the mysterious traveling shop.

They rode and rode, passing through rows of olive trees with silver leaves that sparkled in the bright sunlight. After a few hours, they saw what looked like an old city in the distance. Around the buildings of the city was a high stone wall that kept the city safe. Inside the walls, they could see the roofs of churches, mosques, and synagogues, where people went to pray. They entered the city through one of its nine large wooden gates. As they entered the city, they heard someone chanting aloud. They followed the sound through the city and saw that the sound was coming from a man standing at the top of a very tall tower.

What was he saying?

Still riding the camel, Laila looked through the pages in Grandpa's book. "That tower is called a *Minaret*," she said. "It's part of the Great Mosque of Aleppo. That man is reminding people that it's time to pray. He does it from up high so everyone can hear him."

"I wish I could go up there!" said Ahmed, imagining what he might say if he could get everyone's attention from so high up.

Just then the camels stopped, unexpectedly, in front of an arched wooden door that led into a long, winding market. They knelt to let the children off. The sign above the old door said *Souq Al-Madinah.*

"I guess this is our stop!" Laila laughed.

"Either that or the camels are hungry. I know I am," said Ahmed, sniffing the air. "Hmm...can you smell that, Laila? It smells like roasting nuts."

Laila took a whiff. It smelled delicious. "Wait, I know where we are!" she said excitedly. "Ahmed, do you remember how Grandpa would talk about the famous *souq* in Aleppo, the old market?"

"Umm...not really," said Ahmed, who was still distracted by the yummy smell.

"Oh! You never listen to me, and you never listened when Grandpa told his stories, either!" Laila huffed.

"I do listen, sometimes," said Ahmed with a chuckle. "Maybe I'll remember when I see it."

EIGHT

They jumped off their camels and walked toward the market. It was filled with little shops. Some sold sweets. Some sold spices. Some sold soaps and perfumes. All the shops were squeezed next to each other in a maze with a long and winding path through the middle.

"Oh my!" said Laila. "Just look at all these things. I can't believe it!"

Ahmed liked the winding path. "I want to try everything. Just look at all those treats!" he said, as he ran off ahead of Laila. He ran from shop to shop, stall to stall, laughing with the jolly shopkeepers and tasting their delicious treats.

"Slow down, Ahmed, you're going to crash into something!" Laila shouted, trying to catch her breath and not wanting to let him out of her sight.

She was right. He ran so fast, without looking where he was going, that he crashed into a small wooden wagon. *Thud*—he fell to the ground. "Argh... wh—what was that?" he groaned as he got to his feet, rubbing his throbbing head.

He looked at the wagon and saw it was being pulled by a donkey. Inside the wagon were all sorts of things to eat, but mostly he could see seeds and nuts for sale in small baskets. "It can't be," he whispered to himself as his eyes grew wide. "Laila—Laila! I found it!" he called. "Look! It's a *traveling shop*!" He rubbed his head again, recovering from the bump.

Just then the shopkeeper came around. "My dear boy, this was all my fault. Are you okay?"

"I'm fine, thank you. I wasn't looking where I was going. I just have a little lump on my head." Ahmed smiled up at him.

"I'm so sorry about that." The shopkeeper covered his face. "Help yourselves to some nuts and seeds. It's the least I can do." He held out his hand and led them to the front of the wagon where there were barrels of nuts and seeds of all different sizes. "Try a bag of pistachios. We are famous for these sweet pistachios here in Aleppo. Take some seeds, too."

"It's okay. We are not hungry, and we really must be on our way," Laila responded, in a rush to find their next clue.

Ahmed looked at the bags of nuts. One of them had something shiny peeking out. "Actually sir, may we have that one there?" He pointed to a bag in the very back of the wagon.

After a few minutes of shuffling and searching, the man handed Ahmed the bag.

"Thank you so much!" yelled Ahmed.

Laila was becoming more and more impatient. "Ahmed, all you care about is food! We have a clue to find, remember?"

"Well, that might be true, but look! I think I found our next clue." He pulled the golden note out of the bag and handed it to Laila.

"Oh wow. I didn't expect that," Laila said. *Was Ahmed a better adventurer than she was? He didn't even want to leave home before this.* She was beginning to doubt herself.

"Yeah, but I had to find it the hard way," Ahmed joked, still rubbing his head.

"You're so funny." Laila laughed as she took the note and read it aloud:

Your next clue is spinning round and round, hanging high above the ground.
It helps farmers water their plants and trees, and will cool you off with its gentle breeze.

"Oh man, another riddle?" Ahmed sighed. "At this rate, we will never get home. Why can't this be easier? I need a snack." He munched on some crunchy pistachios.

"Grandpa believed in us and so should you," said Laila. She tapped her finger on her cheek. "Hmm... now, let's think about this together. What spins around and around?"

"Umm...a toy train?" Ahmed guessed. "Or a merry-go-round...hmmm...maybe a Ferris wheel..." He began to daydream about playing with all these fun things.

"Hah!" Laila clapped her hands together. "That's it, Ahmed. You're a genius!"

"I am?" Ahmed scratched his head, confused.

"Yes, a wheel—a wheel that waters plants and trees...a—a waterwheel!" Laila flipped through the pages of Grandpa's book. "Aha—here it is! In the city of Hama there are famous waterwheels that are hundreds of years old. They are built in a river." She showed Ahmed the picture and giggled. "Ahmed, you're getting smarter by the minute."

"Then off to Hama we must go," Ahmed said, happy because Laila thought he was smart.

They ran back to the entrance of the market and jumped onto their camels who, sure enough, knew exactly how to get to Hama.

•• NINE ••

Their journey continued through the desert, under the hot sun. When would they get there?

But before too much longer..."I see it!" said Laila, looking up ahead, using her hand to make shade for her eyes. "Look—I think that's a river behind those trees. That *must* be Hama."

Finding a shady place for their camels to rest, Ahmed and Laila jumped off then made their way to the water.

Clank, clank, clank—they heard a strange noise coming from somewhere. It grew louder and louder as they came closer to the river—*clank, clank, clank.*

"What's that awful noise?" whispered Ahmed as he hid behind Laila. They tiptoed closer to the sound and peeked through some bushes.

"It's the waterwheels!" said Laila. They watched the huge wheels spinning slowly in the water, clanking, creaking, and groaning.

"Look how big they are: just like a Ferris wheel!" Ahmed gasped. He ran to one of the wheels and began to climb it like a jungle gym. "The note from Grandpa—it must be up here somewhere."

An old lady nearby saw Ahmed and yelled, "Come down from there, boy! That is *not* a toy."

Ahmed frowned and started climbing back down. "I'm sorry. I'll come down. It's just that we need to find a note from our grandpa."

The old lady's expression suddenly changed. "Oh my—you must be Ibn Battuta's grandchildren! I've been expecting you for some time. I see you are adventurers just like your grandfather."

"Well, we are trying to be...that's why we're here. We're following Grandpa's clues," Laila boasted. "But wait—how do you know our grandpa?"

"Everyone knows your grandpa! Why, he is the world's greatest traveler, after all! He spent many years in Syria, and visited my shop many times to eat our special sweets. Your grandfather had quite the sweet tooth, you know." She laughed. "You must come try some, too. Hama is well-known for its sweets." She winked.

"Yes, please—can we?" Ahmed drooled as he thought of more treats, and stepped toward her.

Laila quickly grabbed his arm. "Sorry, but we must get back to our adventure."

"Aww, but I love desserts," groaned Ahmed, kicking the ground with his foot.

"But we will visit again someday, and then you can have all the treats you want," Laila assured him. "Now, we really need to find that note."

"Yes, yes...there's no time to waste," said the old lady. "Oh, what a wonderful day." She smiled. "This is very exciting! Hmm, how can I help?" She scratched her head, thinking. "Well, I believe that what you are looking for is up there, but on that wheel." She pointed to the wheel next to the one Ahmed had first climbed.

"I'll get it!" shouted Ahmed, scurrying up the wheel before anyone could stop him. When he reached the

top, he found the note and waved it proudly for them to see.

The old woman covered her eyes with her hands. "Oooh—I can't look. Please don't fall!"

"Wow, Ahmed, where did you learn to climb like that?" asked Laila, as he carefully climbed back down. *Maybe Ahmed is the real adventurer,* Laila thought, *not me.* This was her dream though, so she had to keep trying.

"One day I'll teach you! Now, let's read the clue," said Ahmed, unable to stand still.

Laila read it aloud:

> *(Dy dearest grandchildren, your next clue awaits in ancient Palmyra: the city of dates.
> Look up to where the green sky is sweet,
> your clue will be shading you from the heat.*

"Well then, Palmyra...here we come!" said Laila.

They turned to say goodbye to the old lady and thanked her for helping them.

"I look forward to your next visit—come back anytime!" she said, waving. *"Masalmeh*—bye-bye!"

Layla and Ahmed smiled at each other as they mounted their camels. "Grandpa sure has a lot of friends!" They chuckled as their camels started the journey to the city of Palmyra.

TEN

As they trotted along on their camels with the strong sun shining above them, Laila read about Palmyra in Grandpa's book.

"Wow—did you know that Palmyra is an oasis? That means it's one of the only places in the desert with water. Many people stop there to rest and drink."

All this talk about water reminded Ahmed that he really wanted something cold to drink.

Soon Laila and Ahmed began to see palm trees that grew high up into the sky. As the camels walked closer, still on the hot sand, the children saw a huge building surrounded by tall columns even higher than the trees. They had arrived in Palmyra.

The children stopped right in front of the building, then climbed off the camel. Laila read from her book again as Ahmed looked up and down, amazed, at the columns and walls of the building. "This temple is thousands of years old, Ahmed. It was ruled by Zenobia, one of the greatest queens of all time," read Laila. "Her kingdom had people from many different backgrounds and religions. She treated them all equally, and so they loved her." Laila closed her eyes and tried to imagine what it would be like to be a great queen.

Ahmed looked up into the palm trees where he saw hundreds of plump dates hanging from the leaves. His tummy began to rumble. "Laila, can we please have a snack? Those dates look *so* good!" he said, rubbing his belly. But Laila was too busy imagining that she was a queen.

"Laila!" Ahmed shouted to get her attention.

"You mean *Queen* Laila," she corrected him with a smirk. "Yes, I give you permission to have some dates," she continued as she held out her hand for him to kiss, pretending to be a real queen.

"Very funny," said Ahmed, "now back to the dates."

Laila looked up the gigantic palm tree. "They are so high up. How will we even reach them?"

"What? Have you forgotten that I'm an expert climber?" Ahmed laughed and scurried up the tree. Nothing could stop him when it came to food.

"Hey—grab a few for Mama and Baba, too!" Laila yelled from the bottom of the palm tree.

"Good idea," said Ahmed as he started picking the golden-brown, squishy dates. "One for Mama, and one for me." He smiled, popping one into his mouth. "One for Baba, and another one for me." He giggled, popping another into his mouth. They were the sweetest and most delicious dates he had ever tasted. By the time he climbed down, both his pockets and his mouth were full of dates.

"My mfwant msomthing mo mfrink..." he mumbled.

"What?" Laila laughed. "I can't understand what you're saying while your mouth is so full!"

Gulp—Ahmed swallowed the dates. "I said...I really want something to drink."

"Hmm..." As Laila thought about where to find a drink, she saw a man nearby who looked like he was milking a camel. She had never seen such a thing before. Sure, she had seen someone milk a cow...but a camel?

ELEVEN

"Let's try milking our camel, too!" Laila grabbed the udder at the bottom of the larger camel and pulled down, trying to imitate the man next to them. Milk started to squirt everywhere, on Laila, on Ahmed, and even on the man nearby!

"Hey! What do you think you're doing?" said the man, with a stern look on his face.

Laila hung her head low. "We...we are so sorry. My brother ate too many dates and is thirsty. We wanted to milk our camels like you, but we've never milked a camel before. We've never milked anything before."

The man's stern expression softened to a smile. "You want to try camel milk, do you? That's a good choice because it's the healthiest, creamiest milk ever." He put his hand to his chin. "How about I show you how to milk your camel without splashing your neighbors." He let out a jolly laugh. "First, you need a bowl, then you must tug ever so

gently…" In no time they each had a refreshing cup of camel milk to drink. They thanked the man and began to drink.

"Yummy," sighed Ahmed, gulping away. Laila giggled at the giant milk moustache that was now on Ahmed's top lip. Then she jumped to her feet. "Ahmed, we're having so much fun, we've almost forgotten about our next clue."

"Yes, but the clue is very confusing," sighed Ahmed. "The sky is *never* green and *never* sweet." He looked at the ground then looked up with excitement. "Unless you're climbing a tree and eating dates…"

"That's it!" Laila jumped up and down. "Oh, Ahmed, you've done it again! The sky *does* look green when there are trees! And dates—dates are *always* sweet! Our clue must be with the dates."

Together the children looked up into the trees at the huge leaves that had been shading them all this time. But there were so many trees…hundreds, maybe even thousands.

"How will we know which tree it's in?"

"Eeny-meeny-miny-moe…" Ahmed closed his eyes and pointed at each of the trees, one at a time.

"You must be joking, Ahmed! We don't have time to waste. We have to check every tree." They walked and searched through the trees. After hours they still had not found the clue. They were exhausted.

Laila's lower lip began to quiver, and her eyes filled with tears. "This is too hard. I have no idea what to do. We will never find the clue in all these trees. Ahmed, I thought I was meant to be an adventurer like Grandpa, but maybe I was wrong."

The man who had helped them earlier walked by and overheard her. "My girl, remember Queen Zenobia? No one thought she could rule an empire. She was young just like you, and she became one of the greatest queens of all time. She ruled over this entire city from high above, on the hilltop. No one believed she could do it except…"

"Except she believed in herself." Laila remembered the story, and wiped the tears from her cheeks.

"Precisely."

If I was the queen, I could command my subjects to find the clue, Laila thought. She closed her eyes again and imagined ruling over the entire city from the hilltop. From high above, she could see the tops of all the beautiful buildings below, the desert sands, and all the trees. Her eyes opened wide, and she turned to Ahmed. "I think you can see the tops of all the trees from the hill! And if we can see the tops of all the trees..."

"Then we can find the clue!" Ahmed finished her sentence. The two of them sprinted up the hill before Laila could say another word. The sun was setting. From high above they could see the tops of all the palm trees in the desert.

"There it is." Laila pointed. Down below was a shiny note on top of a long spiky leaf of a palm tree.

Ahmed climbed the tree and grabbed the paper, then handed it to Laila to read:

> Beloved grandchildren, continue your search,
> your next clue waits in Syria's oldest church.
> Look out for a man dressed all in black:
> he will be sure to keep you on track.

"Laila!" squealed Ahmed. "I know this one!" He took Grandpa's book from her and opened it to find a special page. "Here," he said when he found it. "Syria's oldest church is Saint Sergius, in the Christian village of Maaloula. It says here that it's one of the oldest churches in the world."

Laila looked at Ahmed in surprise. "How did you know that?"

"Sometimes I paid attention to Grandpa's stories, too." Ahmed laughed. And with that he raced over to the camel and jumped on. "To the village of Maaloula, please!" he said, almost dancing on the camel with excitement.

Laila looked at him from the corner of her eye. *Hmm—is this the same Ahmed I live with at home?* she thought.

And onward they went. Of course, the camels knew just which way to go.

·· TWELVE ··

The camels strolled along, stumbling and staggering when the ground was rough, until they came to a rocky mountain with tiny, colorful houses bulging out from the sides.

"Are those houses?" Ahmed asked. "I wonder if people live in them?"

"Houses and churches, I think," said Laila, craning her neck to take a closer look. "The church of Saint Sergius must be one of them. Come, let's go see."

They jumped off the camel and headed through a narrow pathway between the mountains. It led them up and up and up, right to the village of multicolored houses and churches.

They wandered around and visited more buildings than they could count. They searched and searched, but couldn't find the church. After a while, Laila said, "I think we need to ask someone for directions." As she was looking for someone to ask, she heard a familiar sound in the background—*ding, ding, ding.* "Wait, what's that sound?"

"It sounds like a school bell, but I don't see anyone in school." Ahmed was stumped.

"Me neither. But you know what other places have bells that ring?"

"Churches!" Ahmed exclaimed.

"And where there's a church bell..."

"...there's a church!" Ahmed interrupted, excited. Laila and Ahmed followed the sound up the hill, between the houses, over the winding road, and straight to the Church of St. Sergius.

"This is it!" Ahmed was delighted. "That wasn't as hard as I thought."

"Now we just need to find the man dressed in black," Laila reminded him.

"Ummm, Laila, I think we might have a problem." Ahmed wrinkled his brow. "*Everyone* here is dressed in black."

Laila looked up, down, and all around. Black here, black there, there was black everywhere! There were crowds of people all around, and almost everyone was dressed in black! "Oh no! This will be impossible." She let out a heavy sigh. "It will take us days to find the right person. Maybe we aren't ready to be adventurers after all."

"Ah, so this clue is too hard for *Queen Zenobia*?" Ahmed teased.

Laila thought for a moment of the brave queen who never gave up. She changed her mind. "Actually, no! We can do this. But I wonder why Grandpa didn't

tell us more. He just said that the man in black will help keep us on track. Who helps people and dresses in black?"

"Baba helps us all the time, and sometimes he wears black." Ahmed laughed.

"Oh Ahmed, always joking around. *Shhhh,* do you hear that?" A voice was coming from within the church. It sounded like a different language. They walked closer, following the sound until they reached a small room lit with candles. The voice was coming from a man. He was surrounded by a group of people in a circle, with their hands clasped tightly together.

"I think they are praying," Laila said.

"That man is helping people pray. I think he's a priest. He helps people and keeps them on track."

"And he's also dressed in black!" Laila finished Ahmed's sentence. "It must be him." The two of them jumped up and down. When the man was finished speaking, the children followed him to the next room. Laila crept up behind him and tapped him gently on his back. "Excuse me, sir..."

The man turned around and looked at the children. *"Sh'lam l-kon!"*

"Sorry?" said Laila, not understanding what the man had said.

"Ah, you're not from here." The man laughed a little. "That means hello in Aramaic, the language we speak here. I'm not surprised you don't understand me. This is one of the only villages in the world that still speaks it. Do you need something?"

"Yes, we wonder if you could help us. We are looking for a clue from a man dressed in black who helps people. Could that be you?"

"Clue?" asked the bearded man. "Hmm—I knew a man once who was always looking for clues. In fact, he wrote them for other people to find, too."

Laila and Ahmed looked at each other with excitement. "That must be our grandpa," they said together.

"You are the grandchildren of Ibn Battuta? My, oh my—what an adventurer he was, and an even better friend. I can see now—yes—you both look just like him!" He put his hand in his pocket and felt around for something.

"Ah...hmmm...aha! Here it is. I have kept this for so long. Now I remember. Your grandfather told me you would come one day. I'm so happy to finally meet you."

"Thank you so much, sir." Laila had a huge smile on her face. She took the note, and read it aloud:

Your journey will end in Syria's heart,
the capital city is where you must start.
Your clue lies in one of the greatest mosques,
at the end of the market's shops and kiosks.

"I don't need the book for this one, it's easy. The capital of Syria is Damascus," Ahmed exclaimed.

"Yes, you're quite right. You're a smart one. Safe travels," said the priest as he disappeared within the halls of the church.

The children waved goodbye and returned to their camels. It was time to visit their final destination.

❧ •• THIRTEEN •• ❧

As they headed in the direction of Damascus, Laila and Ahmed traveled up and down hills until they came to a large mountain.

"This is Mount Qasioun," Laila said, reading a sign on the path as the camel let them down. Both the children smiled as they remembered stories about

this mountain. It was one of their favorites, and Grandpa's, too.

Together they recited a rhyme they had memorized from Grandpa's stories:

Approaching the city, I climbed Mount Qasioun,
gazing across in the light of the moon.
They say great prophets once stood in this place,
admiring the city across time and space.

"This is where legends were made," said Laila, with a warm feeling inside her. She put her arm around Ahmed, and together they peered down in wonder at the beautiful city of Damascus.

"It sure is," responded Ahmed, gazing at the sparkling lights in the distance.

When they finally reached Damascus, they were surprised at how many people filled the narrow streets. They left their camels to rest under a tree then made their way into the marketplace.

Near them another sign read *Souq Al-Hamidiyah*.

"According to the clue," Laila said, "if we just keep walking through this market we should soon find the great mosque."

"And more food hopefully!" said Ahmed.

"Ahmed! You just ate. Besides, don't you still have seeds and dates in your pockets?" said Laila as she walked briskly on toward the mosque.

"Yes, I still have them, but they are for an emergency only." Ahmed smiled, jogging to catch up with Laila. "This is almost like the souq we saw in Aleppo, but noisier and even bigger!" he said, trying not to bump into anyone.

All around them people shopped, ate, and laughed.

Laila and Ahmed walked straight through the market and soon came to the other side. Looking up, they noticed a huge carved archway.

"Is this it?" asked Ahmed. They walked under the tall archway and were surprised to see even more archways on the other side. They were a bit smaller than the first one, and all built of stone.

"Yes, this must be it — the great mosque of Damascus; the oldest stone mosque in the world!" Laila said. She took a few steps closer and touched the walls with her fingertips as she walked.

FOURTEEN

As they entered the mosque, the sounds of the busy market disappeared behind them. Inside was a giant open space without a roof. Birds flew in and out between the pillars and archways around them.

"Birds! I love birds!" said Ahmed excitedly as he ran toward them. Laila did, too, and so their little game of chase began.

The birds knew the inside of the mosque well, and soon the children had been led to just about every corner they could see. Panting from running so fast, they stopped at a tall structure—a pillar that rose high above them.

Ahmed panted, trying to catch his breath. "Isn't this—isn't this the tower where people say Isa (Jesus) will return?" he asked, remembering one of Grandpa's stories.

"Yes. I think you are right," said Laila, also trying to catch her breath. "Grandpa said it was called the *Minaret of Jesus*. And there…" She pointed across the way. "In the prayer hall is the pillar named after Yahya, or John the Baptist."

Once again, Laila and Ahmed were so excited by everything they saw that they forgot they were looking for their final clue. As they explored the enormous building, one of the birds landed softly on Ahmed's head.

"Hey! I think he likes me!" Ahmed chuckled.

As she laughed with Ahmed, Laila spotted something the bird was holding with its foot. "Look, Ahmed. There's a note—I think the bird has brought us a message!" She tried to reach up and grab the rolled-up piece of paper from the bird's foot.

"I guess our clue found us!" Ahmed giggled.

The bird flapped its wings and flew away to perch on the minaret. "No, wait, where are you going?" Laila leaped up.

"Oh no, now what?" Ahmed sighed. "Come down, please," Ahmed pleaded, looking up at the bird, but it wouldn't budge.

"Our clue is gone forever. It was our last clue. Now we will never complete our adventure or find Grandpa's gift," Laila said, frowning.

"Or go home and see Mama and Baba…" Ahmed pouted. "And I had saved all these dates and seeds for them," he said, munching away to comfort himself.

Laila's eyes lit up. "That's it, Ahmed! The seeds—the seeds in your pocket. Birds love to eat seeds!"

They took the seeds from Ahmed's pocket and scattered them in the courtyard of the mosque. All the birds nearby saw the delicious seeds and flew down to enjoy them, including the bird with the clue.

"There it is!" Laila pointed. As the bird happily pecked at the seeds, Laila crept up behind him and carefully grabbed the note from his foot. "The seeds worked. I got our last clue!"

Ahmed grinned. "Speaking of seeds, I could sure use some food."

"Do you *ever* stop thinking about food?" Laila said, smiling. "Since you did give your seeds to the birds, I guess we have to find something else to eat. We can go to a restaurant and read this note there."

They left the mosque and walked until they reached a part of the city called *Bab Touma*.

There they found an old restaurant. Just like the mosque, the restaurant had no ceiling—they could see the sky above them. They felt a cool breeze as they listened to a man in the restaurant play an Arabic guitar, called an *oud,* while singing. Right in the middle of the restaurant was a tall orange tree.

"I've never seen an orange tree *inside* a restaurant," Ahmed said as they went to sit underneath it.

"You'd better watch out." Laila giggled. "An orange might fall on your head!"

The waiter approached them. "*Ahlan wa sahlan,* what can I bring you to eat?"

"Well, what do you have?" Laila responded.

"Today we have delicious kibbeh, hummus, ouzi, fatteh, mint tea, baklava…"

"We'll take one of everything!" Ahmed interrupted before the waiter could finish reading the menu to them.

"Are you sure you want to order all of that?" asked the waiter. "That's a lot of food."

Laila nodded her head, laughing. "Yes, very sure. We have one hungry adventurer here!"

When they had finished eating, Laila pulled out the note the bird had given them. "I think it's time to read our note, Ahmed."

Ahmed had been so busy eating that he had, again, forgotten about clues and riddles. "Oh, yes, you're right." He smiled.

Laila read it out aloud:

My gift to you both is a love for this Earth, and thankfulness for all that it's worth. Your travels have served to open your minds to people and places of all different kinds.

"This clue is different from the others," said Laila. "What does it mean?"

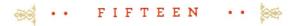

· · FIFTEEN · ·

"No treasure?" Ahmed said. "I thought all adventures had treasure."

"Oh, I see. The adventure *is* the treasure! The gift from Grandpa was our adventure." Laila understood as she remembered all the places they had seen and the people they met. "That is a great gift."

Ahmed remembered the magnificent castle, and climbing the tree and waterwheel. "You're right, it was so much fun."

"But, I guess that means our adventure has come to an end." Laila pouted.

"Don't be sad, Laila. Now you can go home and tell your friends that you really *are* an adventurer, and one that never gives up."

"You mean *we* are adventurers. You solved many clues, too. We did this together."

"You're right." Ahmed smiled. "I did climb up a waterwheel and a palm tree to find our clues. That was fun. And the food, wow! It was all so delicious! I could eat some more."

"Same old Ahmed." Laila laughed. "Except look how brave you have become. And me—one day I'll be the famous Laila Battuta, and I will have traveled to over forty countries, too!"

"Same old Laila," Ahmed sighed, smiling. "Now, how are we going to get home?"

As he said that, the book in Laila's hand began to shake. "Not again." She gulped as she dropped it and stepped back. Ahmed moved away from the book as well. Just as it had done before, the book began to grow bigger and bigger and *bigger*.

"Well, I guess that answers our question!" said Ahmed, this time unafraid.

The book once again turned into a doorway. This time it would take them back home.

"Let's go, Laila!" Ahmed laughed as he grabbed Laila's hand and held on tightly to his dates. With a flying leap, the children threw themselves through the doorway...and down, down and down they fell, tumbling and turning all the way back home. "Goodbye, Syria!" they called out.

SIXTEEN

The children were home in no time. *Plop*—they landed back where their journey had begun.

Laila and Ahmed saw their parents and threw their arms around them, hugging them tightly. Before their parents could even say hello, the children began to chatter on and on about their marvelous adventure.

"Mama, Baba—you'll never believe it. We found Grandpa's journal, and there was a magical door that took us to Syria. We had to solve clues and saw so many different cities..." Laila said, without taking a breath.

"...and we ate so much different food, and fed the birds..." added Ahmed.

"We met so many of Grandpa's friends," said Laila.

"And ate even more food," interrupted Ahmed, as he pulled some dates out of his pockets. "Here, try these. Do we have any camel milk, Mama? It tastes really good with dates!"

"Camel milk? Wait, wait, wait—just *wait* a minute." Mama could not understand anything they were saying. "Just where do you two get your imaginations from? And where did you get these dates?" she asked, looking quite confused.

The sun had set by the time Laila and Ahmed had told their whole story, and their eyelids had begun to droop.

Ahmed stretched his arms up into the air and yawned. "That sure was a busy day," he mumbled as his eyes began to shut.

"Yes, it was," said Laila, with her eyes half-closed as well.

"It sounds like you two had a very interesting day," said Mama, still not believing any of their stories. The children began to prepare for bed. "Ahmed, where is your blanket?" Mama asked.

"I don't need it anymore," replied Ahmed.

"Oh!" Mama replied, surprised. She tucked them into bed, kissed each of them on the cheek, then switched off the light.

Back in the living room, she sat down with a cup of tea, tasting one of the sweet, plump dates Ahmed had brought back. *Hmm...what wonderful imaginations the children have.* She smiled to herself. As she leaned forward to place her cup on the table, she spotted a book underneath it. It was a little torn and covered with sand.

It was Grandpa's journal.

"How did this get here?" She scratched her head. Slowly she began to remember all the stories the children had told her that evening, how tired they had been, and how they had come home with delicious dates and seeds.

"Could it be true? Did the children *really* travel to Syria through a book? But such things are not possible..." She gazed out the window at the twinkling stars. "Or are they?"

Meanwhile, back in the bedroom, Ahmed turned to Laila just as he was about to fall asleep. "Where should we visit next, Laila?" he whispered. But Laila was already fast asleep, dreaming of their next adventure.

The End

For more information and history about the people and sites mentioned in this book, or to learn more about our mission to change the narrative of countries associated with war and conflict, please visit **beneaththerubble.org**

About the Author

Nushin Alloo is a global strategist, writer, and former U.S. diplomat. Born in California, she has lived abroad in Egypt, Lebanon, India, Ghana, the United Arab Emirates, and Syria. She was inspired to write *The Adventures of Laila and Ahmed in Syria* after the start of the Syrian civil war, while working with the country's displaced refugees in Jordan and Greece.

Nushin wrote this book as part of Beauty Beneath the Rubble, a project to help change the narrative of places associated with conflict through the power of storytelling and art. She wants her child and others to learn about and appreciate the beautiful cultures and historical monuments that are vanishing in many conflict areas. Nushin holds master's degrees in Arabic from the University of Maryland and University of Damascus, as well as an MBA from the Wharton School of the University of Pennsylvania.

About the Artist

Shadia Kassem is an accomplished illustrator, painter, and artist. Born and raised in Syria, Shadia graduated with a degree in art from the University of Damascus and currently lives in Kuwait with her husband and two children.

Shadia's paintings have been exhibited in both Syria and Germany. Her enchanting and detailed illustrations fill the pages of *The Adventures of Laila and Ahmed in Syria*. Despite her passion for her heritage and culture, Shadia's own children have not had the opportunity to see their homeland due to the civil war. Shadia hopes that through her illustrations, her children and many others can share her love and appreciation for Syria's beauty and culture.

CPSIA information can be obtained
at www.ICGtesting.com
Printed in the USA
LVRC091454250821
696086LV00003B/112